STEP INTO READING®

STEP 3

Miss Grubb, Super Sub!

A Write-In Reader

by David L. Harrison

____
your name

illustrated by Page O'Rourke

____
your name

Random House New York

The day Mrs. Hoot
stayed home with the flu,
Miss Grubb came
to Pittman School.

Learning to Read and Write Step by Step!

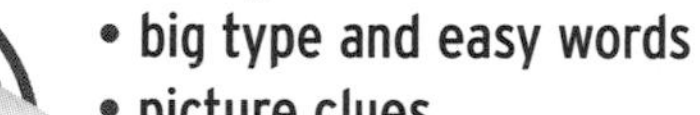

Ready to Read and Write *Preschool–Kindergarten*
- **big type and easy words**
- **picture clues**
- **drawing and first writing activities**

For children who like to "tell" stories by drawing pictures and are eager to write.

Reading and Writing with Help *Preschool–Grade 1*
- **basic vocabulary**
- **short sentences**
- **simple writing activities**

For children who use letters, words, and pictures to tell stories.

Reading and Writing on Your Own *Grades 1–3*
- **popular topics**
- **easy-to-follow plots**
- **creative writing activities**

For children who are comfortable writing simple sentences on their own.

STEP INTO READING® Write-In Readers are designed to give every child a successful reading and writing experience. The grade levels are only guides. Children can progress through the steps at their own speed, developing confidence in their abilities, no matter what grade.

Remember, a lifetime love of reading and writing starts with a single step!

To my friends at Pittman School
—D.L.H.

With love to Griffin and Duncan, my Super Sons
—P.E.O.

 Published in the United States by Random House Children's Books, a division of Random House, Inc., New York, and simultaneously in Canada by Random House of Canada Limited, Toronto.

www.stepintoreading.com

Educators and librarians, for a variety of teaching tools, visit us at
www.randomhouse.com/teachers

ISBN: 0-375-82894-X

Library of Congress Control Number: 2004113154

Printed in the United States of America 10 9 8 7 6 5 4 3

First Edition

The kids of 2B raised an awful fuss.

They even made up a chant.

"Hoot! Hoot! Hoot! Hoot!

We don't want a substitute!"

Miss Grubb clapped her hands.
"I love your chant!" she said.
Then she made up a chant, too.

She beat on a book and yelled,

"Breakfast, lunch, and dinner,

and even in between,

I love to eat pickled beets.

I eat them till I'm green!"

The door opened.
Mr. Tew, the principal,
looked in and waved.
"Is everything all right?"
he asked.
Miss Grubb waved back.
"Perfect!" she said.

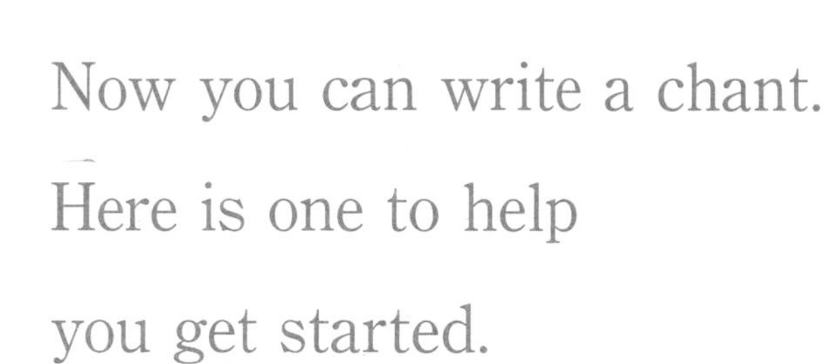

Now you can write a chant.

Here is one to help

you get started.

Yummy, yummy, yummy!

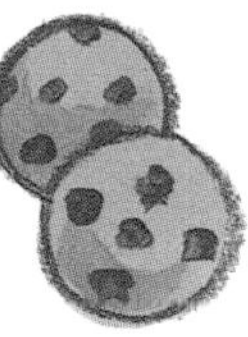

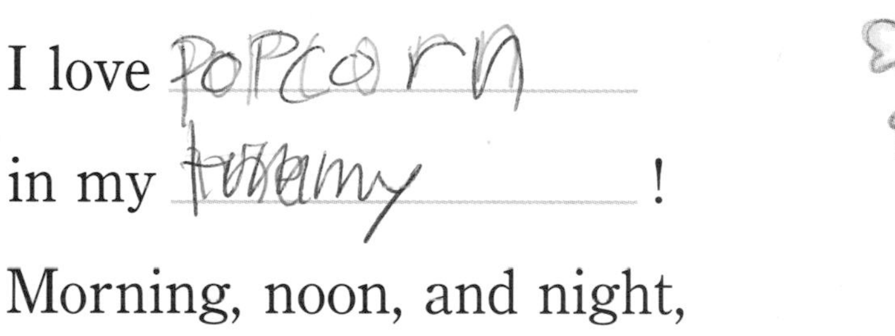

I love popcorn

in my tummy!

Morning, noon, and night,

I gobble every Popcorn [illegible]

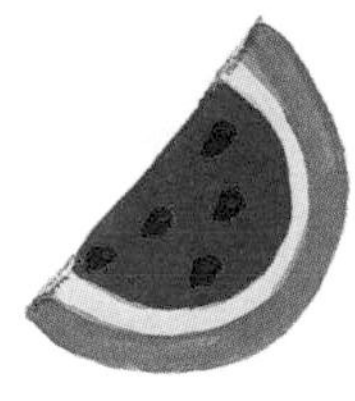

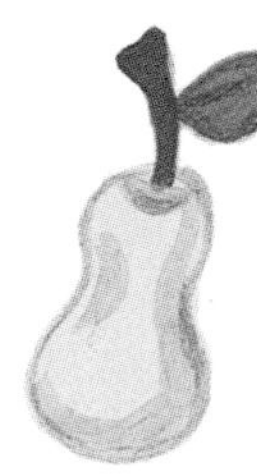

“It’s time for Art,”
said Miss Grubb.
“Everyone into the hall.”
“Why?” the children asked.
“Because that’s where Art is!”
Miss Grubb answered.

Miss Grubb headed to the hall.

The children followed.

Art was the janitor.

He was very busy.

He emptied trash.

He mopped the floor.

He set up chairs.

He cleaned the fountains.

The class drew pictures of him
while he worked.
Miss Grubb clapped.
"Very good Art art,"
she said.

Describe what

your school janitor does.

ne Clenc

Draw a picture of one activity.

Back in Room 2B,
Miss Grubb called,
"Giggle break!
Knock, knock."
"Who's there?" said the class.
"Who-who!" said Miss Grubb.
"Who-who who?" said the class.
The room sounded
like a barn full of owls.
Everyone giggled.

Miss Grubb could use
a little help with her jokes.
Make up a joke of your own
and write it down.

Knock, knock.

Who's there?

Chicken.

Chicken who?

________________.

Q: Why did the Skeleton

cross the road?

A: To thill.

________________!

“It’s time for recess,”
said Miss Grubb.
She handed out paper bags.
“These magic bags can hold
wonderful things!” she said.

Miss Grubb pointed to the sky.
"See that cloud?" she said.
"That cloud goes into my bag.
Hear that robin?
His cheery song goes in, too."

The kids filled their magic bags
with what they saw and heard
and felt and smelled.

Describe something special you would put in <u>your</u> magic bag.
Tell us why you chose it.

Now draw it.

Miss Grubb had more surprises.
"How much math do kids eat?"
she asked the class.
"Kids don't eat math!" they said.

“Mrs. Farmer, the cook, says you do,”
said Miss Grubb.
The class headed to the lunchroom.

“There’s math everywhere,”
Mrs. Farmer said.
She showed them
her weekly food list.
“I multiply and divide
to decide how much to order.”

"Another job is
adding up the money," she said.
"If any is missing,
then we have to subtract!"

The children laughed.
"We do eat a lot of math!"

It was time for lunch.

Mrs. Farmer's food tasted good.

Miss Grubb sat quietly.
She was writing in a journal.
The students asked
what she was writing.
"Wait and see," she said.

Back in class, Miss Grubb
read from her journal.
"Today at lunch,
I heard children's voices.
Tonight when I go to bed,
I will remember the sound.
It will lull me to sleep."

Pretend you are
in Miss Grubb's class.
What would you write
in your journal
about eating lunch at school?

"Want to meet a monster?"
Miss Grubb whispered.
"Where?" the kids asked.

"Right on your hands!"
said Mrs. Teeling.
It was the school nurse!

Mrs. Teeling smiled.
"To meet a monster,
look at your hands."
She said that germs
are monsters so small
they can hide on skin.

She showed everyone
how to scrub their hands
with soap and water.
"We don't want monsters
hiding on you!" she said.

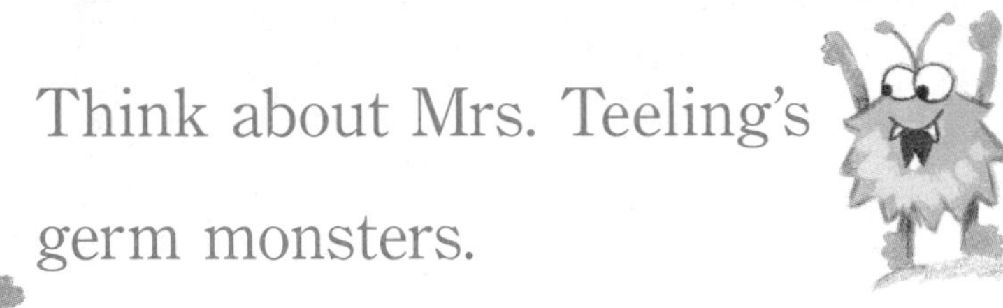

Think about Mrs. Teeling's germ monsters.

Draw one the size of a gorilla!

Then finish this story.

The Day of the Giant Germ

One day a giant germ walked into school. Kids yelled. Teachers yelled. Everyone was afraid! But this is what happened next.

____

____

____

____

____

____

The giant germ was never seen again. Everyone said that ________________

________________ was a hero!

Later, Miss Grubb promised
to send all the students
on their own special trip.
"Where would you like to go?"
she asked.

Everyone shouted at once.

"The ocean!"

"The mountains!"

"The moon!"

"No problem!" said Miss Grubb.

She took them to the library.

The students told the librarian
where they wanted to go.
Mrs. Lairmore helped them
find the perfect books
to take them there.

Miss Grubb winked.
"Won't Mrs. Hoot be surprised
at where you have been?"

Where would you like to take a special trip? Describe that place and explain why you want to go there.

Draw a picture of it.

Back in the classroom,
Miss Grubb asked,
"Can you crack
my spelling code?"
She told the students
to print their names
on pieces of paper

and to make the first letter big.

When she called the students,
they walked to the front
of the room.

They looked like this:

Can you crack Miss Grubb's code?

Fill in the blanks with

the first letter

of each child's name.

___ ___ ___ ___ ___ ___ ___ ___ ___

What does it spell?

Read it out loud!

At the end of the day,
Miss Grubb and the class
wrote notes to Mrs. Hoot
on the board.

“I will never forget you,”
said Miss Grubb.
“I put your sweet faces
into my magic bag.”

The kids all cheered.

They made up a new chant.

“Grubb! Grubb! Grubb!

We love our super sub!

We think you’re super cool!

Come back to Pittman School!”

Everyone agreed.

It had been a perfect day.